Tanner

Stop!
Before you turn the page —
Take a piece of paper.
Pick up your pencil.
Draw a big triangle.

At the top point of the triangle write **Secret Government UFO Test Base**. At the left point write **Dinosaur Graveyard**. At the right point, **Humongous Horror Movie Studios**. And in the exact center of the triangle write Grover's Mill.

Ah, Grover's Mill. A perfectly normal town, bustling with shops, gas stations, motels, restaurants, and schools. A small town with a great big heart, nestled snugly in the midst of —

Wait! Did we say normal? A studio where they film the cheapest horror movies ever made? The world's largest and smelliest graveyard of ancient dinosaur bones? A secret army base filled with captured alien spacecraft?

All this makes poor Grover's Mill the exact center of supreme intergalactic weirdness!

Turn the page.
If you dare.
Enter The Weird Zone!

THE BEAST FROM BENEATH THE CAFETERIA!

THE WEIRD ZONE

THE BEAST FROM BENEATH THE CAFETERIA!

by Tony Abbott

Cover illustration by Broeck Steadman
Illustrated by Peter Peebles

A
LITTLE APPLE
PAPERBACK

SCHOLASTIC INC.
New York Toronto London Auckland Sydney

ISBN 0-590-67435-8

12 11 10 9 8 7 6 5 4 3 2 1   6 7 8 9/9 0 1/0

Printed in the U.S.A   40

First Scholastic printing, September 1996

To Debbie O'Hara

Contents

THE BEAST FROM BENEATH THE CAFETERIA!

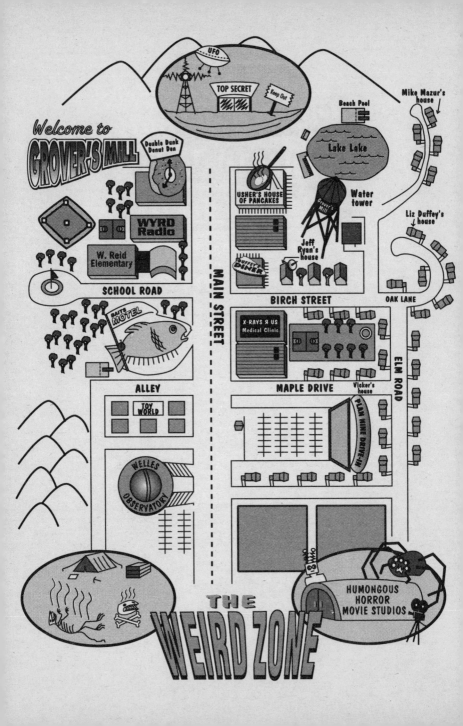

Food, Glorious Food!

Liz Duffey stepped into the lunch line at W. Reid Elementary just in time to stop a disaster.

Mike Mazur, the new kid, was staring down at the steaming gray lump on his tray.

Slowly he pushed the lump around the tray with his finger. "Man," he said. "I'm so hungry. But, whoa!" He pushed the thing some more. "I don't know about this . . ."

Finally, he looked over at Liz and whispered. "What exactly *is* this thing?"

Liz smiled. "You're new here, right?"

"Pretty new," Mike said.

"Rule number one," said Liz. "Always

read before you feed." She pointed to the menu taped on the wall behind them.

Mike squinted up at the sheet of paper. "This can't be right. *Hambooger? With spackle sauce?*" He looked back at the gray lump and frowned.

Liz chuckled. "If Miss Lieberman typed the menu, it's probably supposed to be *hamburger with special sauce*. But you never know, because . . ."

Mike stopped listening when he heard the word *hamburger*. He liked the way it sounded. He looked at the lump again and smiled.

If he had been listening to what Liz was saying, he would have learned a thing or two about W. Reid Elementary School.

A place where, if two things could happen — a regular thing and a weird thing — the weird thing would happen. No contest.

If Mike had been listening to Liz, he would also have heard how Principal Bell always popped up at the oddest moments. And how Miss Lieberman, the assistant principal, was never far behind.

And he would have heard Liz explain that Mr. Sweeney, the janitor, was always angry. And that he didn't like kids. At all.

This was all because their school was in Grover's Mill. And Grover's Mill happened to be the exact center of total intergalactic weirdness.

Finally, if Mike really had been listening, he would have figured out that if the menu said *hambooger*, maybe, just maybe, that's what it really was!

"The Weird Zone," Liz said. "That's what I call it. And the grown-ups that live here are all *Zoners*. Some of the kids are, too."

While Liz was busy explaining all this, Mike was busy picking the gray lump off his tray again and looking at it closely.

He lifted it toward his mouth. "Doesn't look so bad." He smiled. Then his eyes glazed over. "Must feed the stomach," he droned.

He opened his jaws wide.

Suddenly — *fwing!* — Liz's hand flew up and grabbed Mike's arm in midair. She clutched tight and wouldn't let go.

"Don't do it!" Liz cried.

"Must feed the stomach . . ." Mike repeated, tugging hard against Liz's grip.

A big dollop of green drippy stuff oozed out of the lumpy thing in Mike's hand and splatted on the lunch tray. It hissed when it landed.

"I'm losing the spackle sauce!" Mike yelped.

He tugged harder. Liz had to wrestle him with both hands. The gray lump edged closer to Mike's lips. It was almost there.

"Psss . . . psss!" Liz whispered something into Mike's ear.

His arm went limp. He dropped the thing back on his tray. "Really?" he said softly.

Liz nodded. "Believe me, my mom used to work here. This is the stuff that killed the dinosaurs."

HAMBOOGER
WITH
SPACKLE
SAUCE..

Liz pointed to a small trapdoor on the floor just behind the food counter. "Down there in the storage cellar. That's where they keep all the *special* ingredients. Trust me, this place is weird. With a capital *W*."

Mike stared down at the trapdoor. "Thanks," he said. "You saved my life."

Liz smiled. "It's okay. You're new here. But I'll tell you something else about this school," she whispered, pointing to the trapdoor. "My mom said someone has been messing with — "

BANG! The hall door flew open behind them and a dark shadow fell over the lunch line.

"What are you telling this lad, young lady?" a voice boomed.

It was Principal Bell, standing in the doorway with his hands on his hips, staring down at Liz.

He always did that. He loved to stand in doorways with his hands on his hips and stare down at kids. Actually, he was really tall, so he stared down at everybody.

Well, not everybody. He didn't stare down at Miss Leiberman. She was tall, too. And Mr. Bell liked her. His eyes went kind of soft and wimpy and he always stuttered when he saw her.

"Sorry, Principal Bell," said Liz.

"Move along then," he said. "I'm sure your classmates would like to sample this fine . . . fine . . . fine . . ."

Liz looked up at Mr. Bell. He was gazing over the steaming food to the other side of the counter. His eyes had a soft and wimpy look.

Liz whirled around. She nudged Mike and pointed.

Yep, it was Miss Lieberman. Standing there in a white apron, dangling a *hog dog* on a fork.

She dropped it on the floor.

Mr. Bell didn't even notice.

Uh-oh, thought Liz. It's gross-out time.

"Mike, let's get out of here before — "

KA-WHAM!

The trapdoor suddenly burst open and an incredibly hairy arm slithered across the floor and grabbed Miss Lieberman's foot!

Careful What You Wish For

"Ahhhh!" screamed Miss Lieberman.

"Ahhhh!" screamed Mr. Bell when Miss Lieberman screamed.

"Yecch!" snorted a voice from the cellar.

The incredibly hairy arm, which was attached to an incredibly hairy man, let go of Miss Lieberman's foot. The hairy man pulled himself up into the kitchen.

The hairy man was Mr. Sweeney, the janitor.

"Yecch!" he said again. "You kids! You've been raiding my storage cellar again, haven't you?" He shook his finger at Liz and Mike.

Mike looked at Liz. Liz looked at Mike.

They both made faces. "Us?" they mumbled.

"Pah!" Mr. Sweeney snorted. "Such a mess down there! Every day it's worse and worse. Oh, why must I have kids in my school?"

Mr. Sweeney always called W. Reid *his* school.

"But, excuse me," began Principal Bell, "everyone knows it's *my* schoo — "

Thwump! — Mr. Sweeney flung a ripped-open bag of potatoes onto the floor.

The potatoes were *very* rotten. A really bad stink filled the kitchen just as Liz's best friend Holly Vickers jumped into the lunch line.

"Pee-yew!" cried Holly, looking at the sack of potatoes. "Didn't we have that yesterday? Guess I'm skipping lunch again." She made a face and ran from the kitchen straight into the cafeteria.

"Good advice!" breathed Liz. "Come on, Mike. I've got a couple of apples in my backpack."

Liz pushed open the swinging door and —

FLASH! The air exploded in a bright white light!

"Ahhh!" cried Liz, staggering back and nearly knocking Mike and his tray to the floor.

"Yearbook photo!" screeched a voice.

When Liz could see again, she made out the shape of a tiny woman with frizzy gray hair. There was a little black camera where the woman's face should be.

"Mrs. Carbonese!" gasped Liz, blinking. "You, uh, scared me!" Mrs. Carbonese was Liz's teacher. It was her job to take pictures for the W. Reid yearbook. It was called *The Reider's Digest*.

"See you in assembly!" Mrs. Carbonese said. "And don't forget the writing contest, dear." Then she scuttled off to surprise some other students.

Mike squinted into the screaming crowd. He turned to Liz. "Your mom used to work here?"

"Yeah," said Liz, blinking and stumbling her way across the room, "but she escaped. She opened up a restaurant on Main Street called Duffey's Diner. She started with regular food. Now she's changing to health food. Cauliflower steak, broccoli soup, stuff like that."

"Oh, cauliflower steak." Mike made a face. "Interesting. Does your dad work there, too?"

Liz spotted Holly Vickers' dark wavy hair and headed for it. "My dad's a paleontologist who digs up bones for museums. He works at the old dinosaur graveyard outside of town."

"Cool!" said Mike, as they reached the table.

Liz sat between Holly and her brother Sean and across the table from Jeff Ryan.

"Hey, guys," said Mike. He set his tray down on the table next to Jeff and lifted his hand to Sean. "How's it going?"

Sean grinned and slapped Mike's hand.

"Excellent, since I saw you five minutes ago."

Jeff looked over at Mike's tray. "Whoa! You actually ordered the hambooger!"

"And he's not eating it," said Liz sternly. She pulled two shiny green apples out of her backpack and gave one to Mike.

"Thanks," said Mike. "But apples don't do it for me anymore. After being shrunk to the size of a nickel, I'm only interested in one thing — to eat and stay big."

"That's two things," said Liz. "Which reminds me, I'm starting a list right now. I'm calling it — Stuff That Needs to Change." She pulled a pad out of her backpack and started to write. "Number One. No More Weird Lunches."

"I totally agree," said Sean, pulling a blue candy eyeball from his lunch bag and popping it in his mouth. His father, Todd Vickers, was a horror movie director. He had lots of movie props. Some of them were edible.

"Number Two," said Liz. "No Horror Stuff."

"You and Mr. Bell," said Holly. "Mrs. Carbonese, too. They're trying to ban scary books from school. That's what the assembly is all about."

Sean turned to his sister. "But do they know Dad's coming in to film some school scenes for his next horror movie?"

"Sean!" cried Holly. "It's a surprise!"

Liz curled her lip at her friends then looked at Mike. "Zoners? Yes, I think so."

Mike laughed. "You know, it's all how you look at it. I don't think this place is as weird as you guys think it is. I mean, show me weird!"

Sean grinned. His teeth were blue.

"Oh, gross!" Then Liz put down her pen and stared out into the hall. "Uh . . . guys?"

Everyone at the table turned to the door.

It was Principal Bell.

He was standing in the doorway. He was holding the American flag in his hands.

Tears were streaming down his cheeks, like little rivers.

"Mike," whispered Liz. "You wanted weird? Your wish has just been granted."

Mr. Bell staggered into the cafeteria, holding up the flag. "I . . . I . . . I . . . can't . . . !"

He pointed out the door and wept.

There, in a little grassy circle in the center of the parking lot, stood the flagpole.

Except that it wasn't a flagpole anymore.

It was a — flag pretzel! The long silver pole was twisted into a horrible knot.

"Whoa!" muttered Jeff. "Who would do that?"

"Oh, my school!" sobbed Mr. Bell. Miss Lieberman came running from nowhere to comfort him. They stumbled back to the kitchen together.

Liz snapped her fingers. "You know, guys, a lot of strange things have been going on here."

"This is *news*?" said Sean.

"No, listen. My mom heard from her lunch-lady friends that something's getting into the food cellar under the kitchen."

"Maybe it's mice?" said Mike. "We had mice in my old school."

"No way," said Liz. "I'm talking about big stuff. Huge school-size packs of hot dogs and — "

"Hog dogs," mumbled Jeff.

"And bags of french fries," Liz went on, "and hamburger meat, and big tubs of nacho cheese. But my mom said the worst part was — was — "

"Fooood," said Mike, running a finger in the sauce on his burger and lifting it to his mouth.

Wham! Liz pinned Mike's hand down and pushed the apple at him. "If you have to eat, eat something healthy!"

Mike glared at the apple as if it were poisonous. "But . . . but . . ."

"You guys aren't listening!" Liz cried. "I'm talking about a gigantic gross food mess under the school! It's disgusting. Raw meat and gloppy cheese and mushed french fries and rotten — "

Mike, Jeff, Sean, and Holly stopped eating and held their hands over their mouths.

Liz smiled. "Now that I have your attention, I'll tell you something else I heard — "

Eeeeiiiioooaaaccch! A horrible screech echoed down the halls!

It was coming from the gym.

A Surprise Guest

In an instant, Liz, Mike, Sean, Jeff, Holly, and exactly two hundred ninety-four other kids stampeded from the cafeteria down the hall to the gym.

They entered the big bright room.

The wood floor gleamed under the noon sun.

"Something's wrong," whispered Liz.

It was Mr. Gilman, the coach. Normally he would be scribbling on his clipboard and checking kids off one by one as they came through the door — Duffey Liz. Mazur Mike. (He always called everybody by their last names first.) But he wasn't doing any of that now.

Mr. Gilman was standing in the center of the floor. His clipboard was lying at his feet. His face was all twisted. And he was pointing.

Up.

Liz followed his shaking finger. Then she gasped. Everyone gasped at what they saw.

An enormous, jagged hole was torn out of the gym ceiling. Sunlight flooded into the big room. Birds fluttered around the hole.

"Air-conditioning," said Holly. "That's new."

"But who would do that?" muttered Jeff.

"Guys," said Liz, "this place is definitely weirding out. I don't know what it is, but I think we've got trouble. Big trouble in our school."

"*My* school!" screeched Mr. Sweeney as he entered the gym.

Mike gazed up at the giant hole in the ceiling. "We didn't have a sunroof in my old school."

"Ahem!" boomed a voice.

It was Principal Bell. He was standing in the doorway with his hands on his hips, staring down at everybody. He stepped to the center of the gym, right under the jagged opening in the ceiling.

"I am shocked by what is going on in this school and I want everyone to know that I will — "

Splat!

A fat drop of something wet fell on Mr. Bell's head from above.

Slowly, he looked up.

Splat! Splat!

Two more drops fell, this time on his nose.

Liz looked closely at the stuff on Mr. Bell's face. It was green and oozy. It smelled bad.

The glop had dripped from the jagged edges of the hole in the ceiling.

"Oh, go finish your lunches!" cried Mr. Bell, as Miss Lieberman came running out of nowhere with a towel. "Be in the audito-

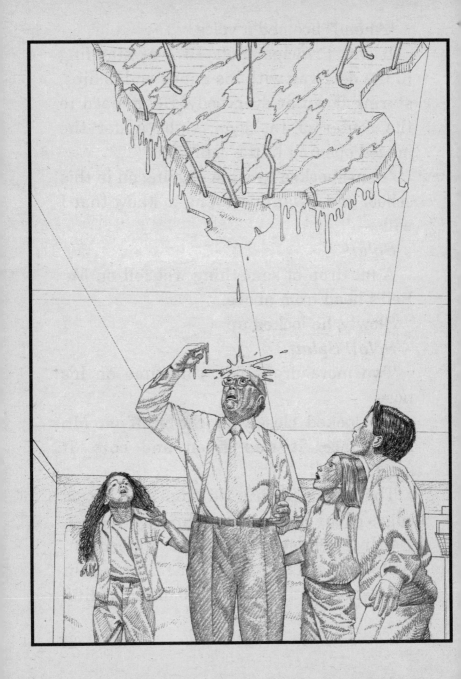

rium for my reading program assembly. I'll deal with you there."

Whoom! In a flash two hundred ninety-eight kids roared back to the cafeteria.

Mr. Bell and Miss Lieberman stalked back out into the hall. Mr. Sweeney went to get a mop.

Coach Gilman stooped for his clipboard and stumbled into the hall, scribbling and mumbling. "Hole . . . ceiling . . . suspects . . ."

But Liz couldn't move. She stared at the hole in the ceiling, watching the green ooze drip and hiss onto the wooden floorboards.

What is going on here? she thought.

Ripped-open bags of rotten potatoes?

A pretzel for a flagpole?

A sunroof in the gym?

Smelly green ooze?

When Liz stepped back into the cafeteria she was trying hard to make some sense of it all.

She was trying so hard, she didn't notice

right away that something was different. Very different.

The clock said 12:35. Still lunchtime. All the tables were filled. First-, second-, third-, fourth-, fifth-grade kids. Normal kids.

Well, thought Liz, as normal as you could get in this school. In this town.

No, it was something else. Then Liz realized what it was. The kids, nearly three hundred of them, were absolutely quiet. No sound at all.

The cafeteria, jammed with kids, was silent!

"Strange," Liz hissed. "Definitely very straaa —"

Then she saw the reason. Well, she didn't actually *see* it. It was more like she *felt* it. It was the floor beneath her. The floor was humming.

It wasn't humming a tune.

It was — vibrating. A little at first, then a lot. The vibrating turned into rumbling. The rumbling turned into quaking.

Then the linoleum floor tiles began to crack.

And split. And pop.

A bulge heaved up in the middle of the floor.

"This is new," said Liz. Holly, Sean, Jeff, and Mike stepped around the hump and over to her.

Suddenly, the floor itself gave out an awful, grinding, ripping, tearing sound.

KKRRREEEEEOOOWWNNNCH!

Chairs and tables went flying. Everybody ran to get out of the way as the floor burst apart.

And something came out.

The first thing Liz saw was the thing's head.

It was the size of a garbage can. It was green and all scaly, with burning red eyes and a long snout.

Under the snout was an enormous open jaw filled with teeth as long as bananas.

Sean looked over at the head twisting in the hole. He tapped his sister, Holly. "Is that Dad surprising us in one of his monster costumes?"

Just then the cafeteria doors swung open and Mr. Vickers appeared with a movie camera on his shoulder. "Hi, kids. I'm here to film!"

That's when the silence broke.

"Ahhhh!" screamed everyone at once.

Smile!

"**R**RRROOOOOOAAAAAARRRRRRRR!**"

The creature sticking out of the floor blasted up and leaped into the cafeteria.

It was eight feet tall, all scaly, had jagged spikes running down its back to a long thick tail, and clawed feet.

"Whoa!" screamed Sean. "It looks like a dinosaur! Only smaller. And weirder!"

"And here!" yelled Jeff.

The huge scaly head swung around, drooling and snorting.

"It sure is ugly!" shouted Holly.

"It's got way bad breath, too," Mike added, holding his nose and backing away.

They were right. It was ugly. And it did

have bad breath. But worse than that, the ugly, bad-smelling thing seemed to be mad at something.

"*RRRROOOOAAAARRR!*" It booted a table out of the way with a huge clawed foot. The table soared across the room and crashed through the windows into the parking lot.

"Wait, do that again," Mr. Vickers said, dodging behind a water fountain and trying to focus his camera. "I didn't get the best angle."

Whoom! A chair sailed inches away from Mr. Vickers' ear and hit the wall.

"Never mind!" the director yelped.

Suddenly, the creature's tongue unrolled like a party noisemaker. It flicked down into the room and — "*SLURRRK!*" The huge tongue sucked up nearly every single crumb of food from every table, from the floor, even right out of kids' hands!

The suction was incredible.

"Hey! That thing stole my lunch!" cried Jeff.

It stole everybody's lunch!

Hundreds of sandwiches, thousands of potato chips, dozens of hamboogers with spackle sauce, and every other piece of food in the cafeteria got slurped up into the beast's ugly mouth hole.

And with each slurping mouthful the beast grew bigger and bigger. And it blasted its stinky breath farther and hotter with each belch.

"I'm gonna faint!" gasped Jeff, staggering.

But the beast was still hungry. It licked its slurpy jaws and looked around for more food. It stepped toward Liz and her friends.

"Don't you dare, you big creep!" Liz whirled around and saw her two apples still on the lunch table. She grabbed them and chucked them right at the beast.

"Slurp! Slurp!" The shiny green apples disappeared into the beast's giant jaws. He still looked hungry. His red eyes flashed with anger.

That's when everything came together for Liz. The food mess in the storage cellar, the flagpole in a knot, the gaping hole in the gym ceiling.

"There's a beast in our school!" she cried.

"*RRRROOOAAAARRR!*" The monster growled his thunderous growl and lunged at the kids!

"And it's time to move on!" said Mike, grabbing his friends and blasting out of the cafeteria.

Liz ran to the right. Everybody else raced left down the main hall.

But the beast followed Liz — *thwump! thwump!*

"Was it the apples?" Liz cried, when she saw the beast following her. "Because I threw them at you? Was that it?"

"*RRRROOOOAAAARRR!*" said the beast.

"I'll take that as a Yes!" Liz said.

The creature's spiked back scraped the ceiling as it charged after Liz, cutting a gash along the ceiling tiles and popping

the hanging lights. It kept growing bigger and bigger.

When Liz dashed around the corner at the end of the hall, her heart leaped into her throat. There in the hallway, just outside the art room, was a group of kindergartners.

Mrs. Carbonese was crouching in front of them and looking through her camera.

"Yearbook photo!" she said.

"No!" cried Liz. But it was too late.

Thwump! Thwump! The beast skidded around the corner and stopped behind the small class. Its head hovered over the children, dripping oozy green stuff from its open jaws.

Mrs. Carbonese tried to focus and tapped her foot. "Will the big fifth grader in the back row please remove yourself," she said. "This photo is for young ones only."

In a split second, Liz knew that the whole class of five-year-olds would be dino food if she didn't do something quick.

She quickly ran over and tapped Mrs. Carbonese's finger.

FLASH! went her teacher's camera.

"RRRROOOOAAAARRR!" went the beast.

"Run!" went Liz.

"Eeeeek!" went Mrs. Carbonese.

Liz pushed the kids and Mrs. Carbonese back into the art room and shot off down the hall toward the double doors of the auditorium.

Thwump! Thwump!

The beast was right after her.

Aisle of the Doomed!

W*ham!* Liz blasted into the auditorium and down the middle aisle toward the stage.

The curtains were closed and there was a podium out front. Posters taped up on the sides of the stage advertised Principal Bell's new reading program and essay contest.

No Scary Paperbacks! read one poster.

Only Good Books! read another.

Some others had pictures of the kinds of good books that Principal Bell and Mrs. Carbonese wanted the students to read: *Tiny Women*, *The Hidden Garden*, *Charlotte's Net*.

BLAM! BLAM! The double doors at the back of the auditorium blew off and the beast barreled down the aisle after Liz.

"So I'm sorry about the apples already!" she cried, scrambling onto the stage.

"RRRROOOAAAARRR!" growled the beast.

Liz fell against the podium, her back up against a poster with a picture of a growling mutant dinosaur in a circle with a line through it.

"Hey, monster," she yelled out, pointing to the poster. "Don't you know what this means? It means no *you*! So shoo!"

But the look on the beast's face told Liz he wasn't impressed with the poster. The look on the beast's face was one of hunger.

Just then the back of the auditorium filled with shapes. Mike, Holly, Sean, and Jeff moved slowly down the aisle toward Liz.

"Hold on," Holly called out. "We'll help you."

"As soon as we figure out how," added Jeff.

But the beast only growled again, opened its huge jaws over Liz, and lunged at her.

"Nooooo!" she screamed.

Then, suddenly, the monster stopped. Its big red eyes began to roll around. It jerked its head back, swatted its snout, shook all over, and —

Twing! Twing!

Two tiny green apples shot back out of its mouth and hurled through the air right at Liz.

She ducked behind the podium.

Wump! Wump! The apples were caught by two hands appearing from behind the curtain.

Liz looked up. "Principal Bell!"

It *was* Mr. Bell. He stepped out from behind the curtain, looked at the two mushy green things in his hand, and shook his head. "Elizabeth Duffey, how many times have I told you that food is strictly forbidden in the — ”

Before he could finish, he glanced down into the auditorium. He saw the big green creature with the long tongue and spiky scales.

“A visitor!” Mr. Bell shrieked. “But I don’t see a visitor’s pass!”

The principal jumped instantly into action.

“Stand behind me, Miss Duffey,” he cried. He whipped open his jacket, pulled out a little card, and yelled, “Beast, I am ordering you in the name of the Grover’s Mill Board of Edu — ”

That was as far as he got.

The green scaly head instantly lunged, the long tongue flicked out, and — *SLOOOORRP!* — in one slurp, Mr. Bell was gone.

Only his shoes were left.

"*R*RROOOAAARRRRR!*" The enormous green beast bellowed. It swallowed hard and whipped its neck back, gashing a hole in the ceiling.

Then the beast bent over and swung its head slowly from side to side, sniffing at Liz and her friends.

"He's deciding who to eat next!" Mike yelled. "I hope it's not me!" He made a dash from the aisle through one of the rows to a side door.

The beast's big red eyes followed Mike as he stumbled between the seats. It lifted its powerful claws to swipe at him.

"Mike! Watch out!" Liz yelled. Without

thinking, she dived off the stage, jumped over the first three rows of seats, grabbed Mike, and pulled him to the floor in the side aisle.

Whoosh! The beast swiped at empty air.

"Oww!" Mike groaned. "Where'd you learn to tackle like that?"

"I used to be on the softball team," Liz huffed.

Mike was quiet for a second. "But you're not supposed to tackle in softball."

"That's why I *used* to be on the team!" Liz grinned. "Come on, everybody. Let's beat it before we all get tackled by drool boy over there!"

Holly, Jeff, and Sean raced for the hole where the back doors used to be.

Mike didn't have to be told twice, either. In a flash he was leaping up the aisle to the side door.

Liz was right behind him.

But the beast was right behind all of them. It stomped up the main aisle and blasted through the back wall. Not through the back door, through the wall!

Bricks tumbled and scattered as the wall burst.

"RRRRRR!" Thwump! Thwump! The beast kicked cinder blocks out of the way and chased the five kids down the hall toward the gym.

"It's gaining on us!" yelled Sean. "It ate Mr. Bell, now it wants dessert!"

It was true. With each huge stride the dinosaur beast got closer and closer.

"Hurry, or we're history!" cried Jeff.

"Prehistory, you mean!" yelled Holly.

Suddenly — *Wham! Clunkety-clunkety-clunk!*

The supply closet door on one side of the hall flew open. A gray metal bucket on wheels shot out of the shadows and stopped in the middle of the hall. There was a mop sticking out of the bucket.

"Yecch!" cried a voice from the closet. "Such a mess!"

"Mr. Sweeney!" yelled Liz, screeching past him. "The beast is right behind us. And he ate Principal Bell!"

"Yes!" hooted the janitor. "I'm in control now!" He pulled the dripping mop from the bucket as the kids raced past him.

Errrrch! The beast skidded to a stop in front of Mr. Sweeney. It lowered its head. It snarled at the janitor.

"Arg!" the janitor snarled back.

And the fight began!

The beast swatted with its claws, but the janitor twirled to one side and poked the beast's scaly hide with the moppy end of the mop.

"Take that, you school wrecker!"

"Arrrggggg!" roared the beast.

"That's my line!" Mr. Sweeney shouted as he dipped the mop into the bucket again and whipped it up at the beast's face. A spray of dirty water splashed into the beast's big red eyes.

"He's good with that mop," said Jeff.

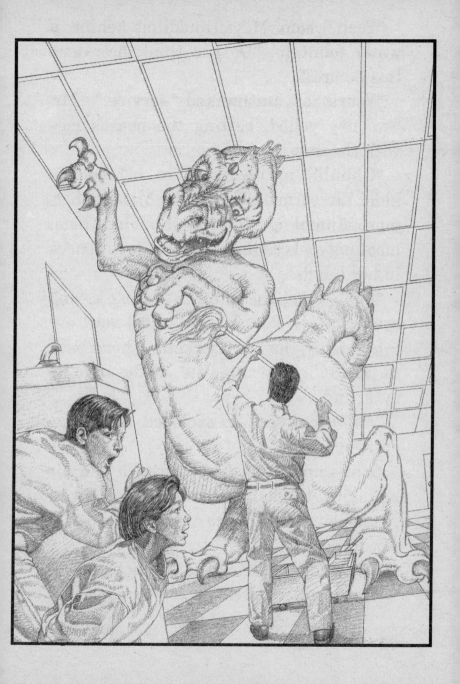

"Yeah," said Mike, huddling behind a water fountain. "Do you think he's done this before?"

"Years of unthanked service!" Mr. Sweeney yelled, batting the beast's legs with the mop.

"Ohhhh!" moaned a voice behind the kids. Liz turned. There was Miss Lieberman, stumbling up the hall behind them, moaning and cradling a pair of goopy shoes in her hands.

"Pah!" cried the janitor. "No use crying over your Mr. Bell. It's my school now!"

Suddenly, the beast jerked its head back to the ceiling, swatted its snout, shut its eyes, and —

"Phhh-toooeeee!" it exploded in a huge spray of green slime!

Something goopy shot through the air and down the hall, screaming all the way. A moment later, there was ooze all over Mr. Sweeney.

"My uniform!" cried the janitor.

"Leonard!" cried Miss Lieberman, run-

44

ning over to the oozy glop all over Mr. Sweeney.

Liz turned to Holly. "Leonard? Who's Leonard?"

"Pah!" snarled the janitor. "He's back again!"

The ooze was Mr. Bell! He was alive!

But he was a mess. "Excuse me, everyone," the principal mumbled. "I've just been in the mouth of — of — that!"

CRUNNCH! The beast whirled around, slamming his heavy tail down on the janitor's bucket. The bucket was as flat as a pancake.

"Without my bucket, I am nothing!" cried Mr. Sweeney. He ran down the hall. Principal Bell and Miss Lieberman shuffled off after him.

The beast stretched, snorted, and punched a hole into the school store. It did another slurping thing with its tongue and ten boxes of candy bars disappeared into its teeth-filled jaws.

"Come on, guys," said Holly, edging away

from the beast. "I think we'd better get out of here while we can." Jeff and Sean followed her.

Liz stood there, gazing at what she was seeing. She knew it was Grover's Mill. She knew it was a zone of total weirdness, the center of everything that's strange in the galaxy. But still her brain asked her, "Hey, what's with the big monster?"

She grabbed Mike by his shirtsleeve and pulled him up to her nose. "A beast, Mike! A huge, scaly, green beast thing in our school!"

"I see it, I see it!" he nodded. "But everybody else is escaping and I wanna go, too."

Too late.

KRACHOOOOOM!

The beast whipped its giant tail down with such force that the front wall of the school toppled!

Sending tons of bricks and cinder blocks crashing down.

Right onto the two kids!

Goo-goo! Ga-ga! GORGA!

Whoosh! Something flashed quickly between the tumbling wall and Liz and Mike.

Liz felt herself being pulled up into the air.

"Hey, we're flying!" yelped Mike.

An instant later, the two kids were standing safely in the gym as the front wall of the school crumbled behind them like toy blocks.

"You kids okay?" said a voice from the swirling dust and crumbling stone.

Before them stood a man. He wore a sun helmet, dusty goggles, brown field pants, and boots. He snapped the handle of a

47

leather bullwhip and it unwound from an overhead light. He coiled it back onto his belt.

"Um, we're not dead," said Mike. "So, yeah!"

The man pulled the goggles up onto his helmet, flipped Liz's hair, and laughed.

Then he put out his hand to Mike. "Duffey," he said. "Kramer Duffey."

Mike's jaw sank to his chest. "Liz, this is your dad? Wow! He looks like, I mean, you look like — you know who!"

Liz knew who. Her father was an adventurer.

A dinosaur hunter. A danger kind of guy.

Kramer Duffey pointed over his shoulder at the beast as it stalked off into the parking lot. "Sent home for bad behavior?"

"He was under our school," said Mike.

Kramer Duffey nodded. "It figures. I found a dinosaur egg deep in a cave and brought it to my tent. The next morning it was just little bits of broken shell and" —

he wiped his forehead with the back of his hand — "then I saw footprints."

CRASH! The beast hoisted an empty school bus in each giant claw and clapped them together like blackboard erasers.

"Footprints?" asked Mike.

"Tiny ones, heading for your school," Mr. Duffey told them. "The other funny thing was the weather that night. A big green cloud came floating across the desert."

"RRROOOAAARRRRR!" The huge beast growled and dropped the crumpled mess of yellow bus metal to the ground like last week's bad spelling test.

Liz's mind began to work. *Clank!* — *Clunk!* — *Fizzz!* It didn't get very far. "But dinosaur eggs don't just hatch after sixty-five million years."

"Weird, huh?" Kramer Duffey said.

"Ahhhh!" Yelling and shrieking came from outside the school.

About a hundred kids were screaming as they all raced out of the building.

Liz turned to see Mr. Vickers running

backward across the parking lot, looking through his movie camera. Sean, Holly, and Jeff were right behind him.

"Excellent screams, children!" Mr. Vickers called out. "But a little more fear around the eyes, please!"

A moment later, they were all gone.

"Wow, that beast knows only one thing," said Mike. "To eat and to destroy!"

"That's two things," said Liz.

"Don't get technical," Mike snapped.

They watched as the beast uprooted the flagpole from the ground and used it as a toothpick.

"I call him Gorgasaurus," Mr. Duffey said. "Gorga, for short. Like it?"

"Gorga . . ." muttered Liz. "It sounds . . . big!"

It *was* big! And just then the big thing tore into some power lines near the school and began to chew them. After that he tramped after a crowd of townspeople who had come to watch.

"Gorga's heading into town," said Mr.

Duffey. He turned to Liz. "You kids take cover. Gotta keep big boy away from your mom's diner."

"But Dad, wait a sec — "

Before Liz could say another word, Kramer Duffey, world-famous paleontologist, dashed into the street, unhooked his whip, and snapped it high. The end curled right around the huge beast's neck.

"Ya-hoo!" Mr. Duffey yelled as Gorga pulled back suddenly and Mr. Duffey went flying up. "See you later, Liz! Nice meeting you, Mike!"

Mr. Duffey swung wide and high over Main Street. He finally let go of the whip over the roof of Duffey's Diner.

"Wow!" muttered Mike. "Cool whip." Suddenly, a frown flashed across Mike's forehead. "Cool whip? Hey, I never ate lunch today."

Liz gave him a look. "Later, Mike. We've got to see where Gorga's going next. Come on!" The two kids dashed up School Road.

Bong! The big clock on top of the Double Dunk Donut Den rang the hour.

Sssss! The oversize pan atop Usher's House of Pancakes hissed the hour.

"RRROOOAAARRRRR!" went Gorga. He stopped stomping and headed for the center of Grover's Mill, drooling at the restaurants.

"Uh-oh," gasped Liz. "He wants a snack. He's going to get bigger again. Let's get out of here!"

But Gorga had other ideas. He spotted the two tiny figures running down the street. He rolled his big red eyes. He licked his long teeth.

The ground thundered.

A dark shadow fell over the two kids.

"Gorga!" screamed Liz. "He's going to squish us!"

*S*plaaaaaaaaaaaaaaaaat!

Well, almost!

Just inches from the two kids, Gorga's enormous clawed foot stopped. A sudden squealing sound pierced the air. Gorga turned to listen.

It was a motorcycle screeching around the corner from Main Street.

And driving the motorcycle was — Miss Lieberman!

"Whoa, she really gets around!" gasped Mike, jumping out of the way.

Miss Lieberman spun to a stop right in front of the two kids. A head popped up from a sidecar attached to the motorcycle.

"Principal Bell!" shouted Liz.

"Don't worry, children" said Mr. Bell, leaping out of the sidecar. He was dressed from head to toe in an army uniform. "We've got an oversized school wrecker on the run!"

Just then, the beast's huge foot slammed down, causing a huge crack in School Road.

"Yeah, on the run!" shrieked Mike. "Not!"

Mr. Bell jumped back into the sidecar. "Miss Lieberman, step on it!"

"Before Gorga does!" yelled Liz.

The assistant principal nodded, pulled down her goggles, and gunned the engine. The motorcycle screeched off with Gorga in hot pursuit.

"And don't forget the writing contest!" Principal Bell called back. "All entries due tomorrow!"

"What was that contest again?" Mike asked.

"It doesn't matter, Mike," huffed Liz. "I don't think we're going to make it to tomorrow!"

In the distance, Liz spotted the domed head of the Welles Observatory. It looked safe. "The Observatory!" she yelled. "It's our only chance!"

"Great!" said Mike. "My folks can help us!"

The two kids took off down Main Street.

Bong! The oversized donut clock on the roof of the Double Dunk Donut Den rang out again.

It was the last time.

In one quick swipe, Gorga tore the thirty-foot clock right off the Den's roof and took a bite.

"SPAH!" Gorga coughed, spitting wood chips and heaving the giant wooden pastry down the street right at the two kids.

"That's another one for my list!" cried Liz, ducking as the donut shattered on the street. "No Big Food Signs!" Two minutes later she and Mike were dashing up the

wide steps of the Welles Observatory and Science Museum.

At the top of the steps, Liz looked back.

Gorga dunked his head through the open roof of the Donut Den, slurped in a mighty slurp of donuts and crullers, and grew ten feet taller.

Then he stomped the Den flat!

"Grover's Mill!" cried Liz. "It's being destroyed stomp by stomp and slurp by slurp!"

"Well," said Mike, "you said you wanted things to change. Come on!"

Sure, thought Liz. She'd even made a list of things to change. But was this what she wanted?

Mike pushed on two giant doors, which opened into a large room with a domed ceiling.

Inside, a man dressed in a white laboratory coat was staring into a giant telescope. Liz recognized him as Mike's father.

"Ah," said Mr. Mazur, shifting his glasses and licking his teeth, which seemed

far too big for his mouth. "Small . . . famil-
iar . . . boy . . . person."

"Mike," said Mike.

"Yes, yes, quite right," the man said. He
pushed a button. *Zzzzz!* — a narrow slit
opened in the ceiling and the telescope
pushed out.

"Gorga's out there, Mr. Mazur," said Liz.
"He's a huge dinosaur and he's wrecking
everything! The whole town! What can we
do?"

The man pulled a long Gooey Bar from
his lab coat, unwrapped it, and began to
munch. "First, let's get a look at the creature, shall we? Science helps us under-
stand all things."

Liz wasn't really sure about that, but it
did make her feel better. Well, a little.

At least until Mike came over and
tapped her on the shoulder. He showed her
his hands. They had greenish powder all
over them.

"Um, Dad?" asked Mike. "What's this
green stuff? It's on everything."

Mr. Mazur chuckled, then fiddled with the telescope controls. "Ah, the green cloud!"

"*What?*" asked Liz, staring in shock as Mr. Mazur pushed his glasses back up his nose. "Did you say a *green cloud*?"

Mr. Mazur nodded. "One of my own experiments, actually. I, ah . . . hmmm. I seem to be quite hungry since that night, actually. Candy, mostly." He reached into his pocket and pulled out another long Gooey Bar.

"That stuff's not good for you," Liz said.

Mike looked at her. "Never mind that. Your father said a green cloud drifted across the desert the night the dino egg hatched, right?"

Liz frowned. "But what does the cloud do?"

Mr. Mazur wrinkled his nose. "Actually, under certain kinds of circumstances, a green cloud can do some very odd things."

"What sorts of things?" asked Liz.

"Well, judging from my own experience,"

Mr. Mazur said, "I'd say, it caused an appetite for food. Mostly candy and sweet things."

"But you can reverse it, right?" asked Mike, trying to wipe the green stuff off his hands.

Mr. Mazur scratched his head. "Actually, your mother has forbidden me to do anymore experiments." He shrugged at Mike. "So you see . . ."

Liz knew this was not good. She stormed back and forth across the big room. "Okay, so a dinosaur — Gorga — gets zapped by this strange cloud. Why? Hey, it's Grover's Mill, that's why. Then he gets really hungry. Well, sure. He hasn't eaten for sixty-five million years. So he comes to our cafeteria. And he snarfs up the hamboogers. Then he goes after candy, then donuts, then he — Wait!"

Mike stopped wiping his hands on his pants and looked at Liz. "Okay, I'm waiting."

It was like fireworks exploding in her

head. In seconds Liz knew the answer. She pulled an apple from her backpack and began to laugh.

"Hey," said Mike, "how many apples do you carry around, anyway?"

"Never mind that," snapped Liz. "The point is — Gorga spat out the apples!"

Mike searched Liz's face, trying to get it. "Of course! Gorga spat out the apples. Yeah, I get it. Wow, that's brilliant, because . . . because . . ." Mike shook his head. "Because why, exactly?"

"Because he only likes junk food!" cried Liz. "School food! Donuts! They make him bigger!"

Mike thought about that. "So, to make him smaller, we do . . . um . . . what?"

Mike's father peered into the telescope. "Actually, Gorgo *is* getting smaller. He's going away."

"Smaller?" said Mike.

"Going away?" said Liz.

"Science never lies," Mr. Mazur said, smiling.

WHAM! A door at the back of the room swung open and a woman in a white lab coat stormed in. "Mortimer!" she shouted. "How many times have I told you — you're supposed to look in the *small* end of the telescope!"

"Oh, dear!" said Mr. Mazur.

That's when Liz realized something horrible. "So you mean, Gorga isn't getting smaller?"

"He isn't going away?" asked Mike.

"RRROOOAAARRRRR!"

Nope. Gorga was bigger.

And Gorga was there!

"*RRROOOAAARRRRR!*" Gorga stuck his big scaly head — now the size of a dump truck — into the slit in the dome. He looked all around.

"He's gonna slurp!" yelled Liz. She grabbed Mike and pulled him down behind the telescope. Mr. and Mrs. Mazur ducked.

SPPPLURRRSSSSSH! All the drawers in all the cabinets burst open and hundreds of packages of candy and chips and other junk food went flying up through the slit and into Gorga's jaws!

"My candy!" yelped Mr. Mazur.

"Mortimer!" cried Mrs. Mazur in disgust.

The suction from Gorga's slurp was even stronger than before.

Liz's bangs flapped up. Her grip started to loosen. The Mazurs' lab coats swirled up over their heads. Mike's feet were leaving the floor.

Liz knew that any second they would all be flying into that huge mouth hole. She had to act.

She did act!

With all her might, Liz reached up and hit a button on the telescope stand.

Zzzz! — the narrow slit in the ceiling closed swiftly on Gorga's neck, trapping his giant head inside the dome!

"ARRGGG!" He gurgled, he pushed, he wiggled, he pulled, he strained. His eyes got redder and bulged. But he couldn't get free.

"Let's get to my mom's restaurant!" Liz cried out. "I have a plan!"

The two kids tore out to the front steps

of the observatory and started for the white and blue awning of Duffey's Diner. "Hurry!" Liz yelled.

But in the middle of Main Street, on its way to the same white and blue awning, was something ugly. Something horrible.

It was a mob! A mob of angry townspeople. They had their eyes on Duffey's Diner. They had torches. They had sticks. They had attitudes. But worst of all, they had a song!

Oh, see mighty Gorga
From the dinosaur ga-
raveyard roar and eat and kill!

"Zoners!" cried Liz. "They're out of control!"

"They're also out of tune," said Mike.

Liz ran. "We have to stop them."

"Yeah," Mike agreed. "Before they get to the second verse!"

No! Too late!

Oh, see mighty Gorga
Stomp till there's no more Ga-
*   -rover's — rover's — rover's Mill!*

Suddenly — *Errrrch!*

Screeching to a stop in front of the diner was a huge army tank. It had BOARD OF EDUCATION stenciled on the side.

A hatch on the tank opened. A man wearing a camouflage army uniform and helmet popped out. He pulled off a foggy pair of goggles.

"Principal Bell!" gasped Liz. "Again!"

"Commander Bell, now," Mr. Bell said. "The superintendent has given me emergency powers. Now listen up, people. Our intelligence experts tell us the beast is after only one thing — food, food, food!"

Liz made a face. "That's three things."

Mr. Bell went on. "However, if there is no food, Gorga will go away. Since he has already destroyed our beloved Donut Den and House of Pancakes, that leaves only one restaurant still standing — Duffey's

Diner! I've sent for attack planes to bomb Duffey's Diner to smithereens!"

The crowd cheered.

"No!" Liz screamed. "You can't do that! We need my mom's restaurant! I figured it all out. There's only one way to defeat Gorga!"

"Explain, Miss Duffey," boomed Mr. Bell.

"Sing a song!" roared the crowd. "We did!"

Liz stepped slowly before the crowd. She thought for a second. Then she began to sing.

Wherever slimy burgers ooze —
Gorga will be there!
Wherever cheeses taste like glues —
Gorga will be there!
One thing alone can stop the beast
From making Grover's Mill his feast
With Duffey's health food you can't lose —
And prices are fair!

"Oooooh!" gasped the crowd. "Good song!"

"It's the best I could do on short notice," said Liz.

Liz's mother and father stepped out of the diner. "We'll do whatever we can," they said.

Then the crowd parted and two very round figures came forward. Two very round, very identical figures.

One of them spoke. "Hi, I'm Bob Dunk and this is my brother Rob Dunk. We're the Double Dunk twins!"

The crowd applauded.

"Thank you," continued Bob, holding back tears. "Even though the Donut Den is no more, we'd like to offer our secret donut recipes to help defeat the beast!"

Everyone cheered again.

"I'll help, too," snarled an angry voice, "if I must!" An elderly gentleman limped out of the crowd and frowned at everyone. It was Mr. Usher, owner of Usher's House of Pancakes.

The crowd cheered again.

"That's the Grover's Mill spirit!" said Mr. Bell.

Suddenly Miss Lieberman popped out through the open tank hatch.

"Did someone say *Grover's Mill*?" She shook a set of pink pom-poms. "Give me a *G*!"

"Geeeee!" roared the crowd.

"Give me an *R*!"

"Rrrrrrr!" roared the crowd.

"Give me an *O*!"

"Rrrrrrr!"

Mr. Bell stared down at the crowd. " 'Rrrrr'? That's not right. Now give me an *O*!"

"RRRRRRRRRRRRRRRRRRRRRRR!"

A small man with thick glasses pushed his way quickly through the crowd. "Ah, actually, the beast creature is coming!" It was Mr. Mazur. And he was pointing.

Gorga was starting to break free of the observatory dome.

Soon the beast would be stomping up

Main Street! At full speed! And really mad!

"Everyone back to school!" Liz screamed.

"Oh, man!" groaned Mike. "And I thought we were out for the day!"

To Eat and to Destroy

As the crowd ran for cover, Liz and Mike dashed down School Road, past the crumpled sign that read DEAD END, and up the steps to the ruined main lobby of W. Reid Elementary.

The tank rumbled behind them along with the whole mob of torch-carrying, stick-toting townspeople.

Holly ran up to Liz and Mike. Sean and Jeff were right behind her. "You guys need some help?" asked Holly. She smiled at Liz.

Liz nodded. "It could be dangerous."

"Cool," said Sean, nudging Jeff. "A mission."

The five friends strode toward the school.

"Halt!" Mr. Bell boomed, jumping from the tank and standing in front of the school doors. "The freedom of the free world is at stake! If you five students fail in your mission, we will be forced to use state-of-the-art nuclear weapons. Life as we know it may end."

Liz frowned. "Oh, no pressure or anything. Could we at least have ten minutes?"

Mr. Bell looked deep into her eyes and smiled. "One second more and we start bombing!"

"Thanks for your support," said Mike.

"Kids, wave!" Mr. Vickers called out from the crowd. He held up his camera. "We're rolling!"

Moments later in the main hallway, Liz was giving instructions to Holly, Sean, and Jeff. "Meet us in the gym in five minutes."

The kids nodded and split up. Liz pulled

Mike with her. In seconds, they were climbing down through the trapdoor to the kitchen food cellar.

At the bottom was Mr. Sweeney, the janitor. He was dressed like a ninja, with cleaning brushes and tools crisscrossing his chest on a wide belt. Mops of all different sizes lined the walls. "Stand back, you little invaders!"

Liz and Mike explained everything.

Mr. Sweeney listened. "My school — a battleground?"

Mike nodded. "And we've only got minutes."

Mr. Sweeney sprung over to a door at the far end of the cellar and led them into a dark tunnel. The tunnel wound through turn after turn.

"Where exactly are we going?" Mike asked.

"Into the depths of my school," the janitor said. There were doors on both sides as they passed. One had a skull and crossbones across it. Another was marked TOP SECRET. Still another said TEACHERS' LOUNGE — SUB-LEVEL ONE.

"I know every inch of the place," Mr. Sweeney went on. "I've lived down here for years."

Liz turned to Mike. "That's a fun thought."

Finally the tunnel stopped at a huge iron door.

Vrrrrt! The door opened to a room jammed with enormous crates of food ingredients.

"My secret underground supply room!" the janitor exclaimed. "My home!"

"Come on, we're running out of time," said Liz, looking around. "Mike, help me choose the ooze. What looks bad?"

Mike's eyes flashed. "What doesn't?" He strode over and tapped a big round drum. "Easy-Cheese, definitely." He pointed to a high shelf. "All-Sauce, of course." He whirled around. "Oh, and lots of this Meat-Treat stuff."

Within minutes, the three had collected dozens of tubs of food stuff. They hauled it all back through the tunnels and upstairs into the gym.

Holly and Jeff came running in with a bunch of mops. Sean pulled in a bucket on wheels.

"My mops!" cried Mr. Sweeney. "My bucket!"

Liz looked up at the jagged hole that she had first seen that morning. The afternoon light shone down on the gleaming wooden floor.

"Okay, guys," said Liz. "Let's get cooking!"

Mike opened the food tubs while Holly and Jeff began to mix the ingredients right there on the floor, using the mops from the supply closet. Sean splashed the mess with dirty water.

The Double Dunk twins came in with a hand truck. So did Mr. Usher. They all brought big containers and mixed their stuff in with the rest.

"This is smelling pretty gross, Liz," said Mike.

"Keep stirring," snapped Liz, looking out the window toward the observatory. "Gorga's nearly unstuck. If this doesn't work, Grover's Mill could be a thing of the past."

Mike nodded. "Yeah, I kind of like it here. Except for Gorga and all."

Liz smiled a half smile. "Yeah, well, just don't become a Zoner, okay?"

Errrrch! The sound of squealing tires from outside. "That's my mom and dad," said Liz. "Mr. Sweeney! Help them back their truck around to the side door. They'll do the rest."

The janitor grumbled as he headed out of the gym. Kramer Duffey backed his big dump truck up to the door.

The goop the kids had mixed on the floor bubbled and changed color. The horrible aroma rose up through the ceiling hole and out into the air.

"All ready over here!" cried Liz's mom

from the back of the truck. "And it's delicious!"

Suddenly — *"RRROOOAAARRRRR!"* The sound of the giant beast echoed across Grover's Mill.

"Gorga's free!" cried Liz. "Take cover!"

THWUMP! THWUMP! Gorga stomped up Main Street and charged across the school parking lot. He dipped his enormous head through the hole in the gym roof and sniffed the goopy mess bubbling in the center of the floor.

"Whoa!" Mike cried. "His tongue's curling!"

"Dig in, big boy!" shouted Liz.

"*SLOOOORRRRLLLPPP!*"

Oh, did the big boy dig in!

The incredible wind of Gorga's humongous slurp made Liz and Mike brace themselves in a doorway.

As Gorga slurped up the soupy mess on the floor he grew bigger! And bigger! And bigger!

"Now the secret weapon!" Liz shouted.

She gave the signal and — *GRRRR!*

Kramer Duffey pulled a lever and the truck at the side door began to tip its load.

"Today's special coming right up!" Mrs. Duffey cried out from the seat next to her husband. "Cauliflower soup with broccoli!"

"Hooray!" Liz cheered. "Health food!"

Mrs. Duffey's health food cuisine splashed out across the floor.

"*SLLLLLLURP!*" Gorga kept snorting and slurping. He didn't notice that the menu had changed!

He swallowed everything. He licked the floor clean. Then he pulled his giant-sized head back and roared. His jaws were trailing broccoli bits and cauliflower stems.

Suddenly, Gorga grew quiet. He licked his jaws with his long tongue.

"He's not liking it," Mike mumbled.

Mike was right. A shocked expression struck Gorga's huge red eyes. He glared down at the little people in the gym. He looked at the Double Dunk twins. He looked at Mr. Sweeney. He looked at Mr. Usher. He looked at Mike, Jeff, Holly, and Sean.

Suddenly, his huge red eyes spotted Liz. He gave her a look.

Liz didn't like that look one bit. "Uh-oh,

he remembers the apples." She ran.

Her head pounded. Her arms tingled. She pumped her legs as fast as she could. "He's not going to get me!" she grunted, trying to make it to the gym doors.

But Gorga was too swift. He slammed his claw down through the ceiling and closed it tight!

Around Liz!

"RRROOOAAARRRRR!" Gorga lifted her in triumph high over Grover's Mill!

"Hellllp!" screamed Liz, swooping up in the air hundreds of feet above the town.

"I hate to lose a student," Principal Bell cried out from the front of the school. "But — send in the attack planes!"

Jaws of Death!
Jaws of Breath!—Bad!

Gorga bent down to examine the tiny girl squirming in his grasp. The beast's claw was rough. His scaly hide was thick, like armor. His breath was not too good, either.

"You're going on my list, too, big boy," said Liz. "No More Monsters in Grover's Mill!"

Gorga's eyes were bulging and rolling around.

Cauliflower juice ran down his chin, mingled with Easy-Cheese. Tiny broccoli bits were stuck between his enormous teeth.

Gorga could have crushed Liz with a single squeeze, but he didn't. He flicked her bangs up and down with a huge clawed finger. He made little gurgling noises.

"Yeah, yeah, I know, my hair," said Liz. "It's a lot of fun. Now, put me down!"

"RRROOOAAARRRRR!" Gorga hoisted Liz high up to the clouds and shook his fist.

"Whoa!" she cried. "I'll take that as a No!"

Suddenly Gorga stopped roaring. He tilted his head like a puppy listening to something in the distance.

Everything was quiet and peaceful.

Well, almost.

Nnnnn! Liz heard a rumbling off in the distant skies. Gorga swung his giant head.

"Planes?" said Liz. "No, it couldn't be!"

Up over the horizon the planes came. Fierce-looking black jet fighters, armed with missiles. Lots and lots of missiles.

"Ah!" beamed Mr. Bell. "The finest attack force a PTA fund-raiser can buy! They'll do the trick!"

"Hey!" Liz shrieked. "I'm up here!"

POOM! POOM! The distant sound of missiles firing from the fighters resounded through the air. Plumes of smoke whirled backward from the tails of the missiles. Lots of missiles!

KA-THOOM! The first missile scored a direct hit on Gorga's shoulder. The beast scratched where it exploded.

"You can't do this!" yelled Mike. "Liz is my friend. She saved my life a bunch of times!"

But the planes circled for another strike.

Finally, Mike shouted, "Don't worry, Liz! I'll save you!" He ran for Gorga's huge clawed feet and began scaling up a scaly leg.

Hand over hand he climbed.

Mike looked up. He wasn't exactly sure what he was going to do. He just knew he had to try.

Then he saw it. Above him, dangling down from Gorga's neck, was Kramer

Duffey's bullwhip. As it swung closer, Mike reached out, grabbed the end of the whip, and pushed off from Gorga's kneecap.

"Yes!" Mike cried out. "Just like the movies!"

As the whip tightened, Gorga arched back and the whip began to coil up around his huge neck. Mike held tight and the whip wound closer and closer to the beast's giant jaws of death!

"Uh-oh, I'm beast food!" Mike shrieked.

"RRROOOAAARRRRR!" Gorga opened his mighty jaws, waiting for Mike to swing in.

"Nooooooo!" yelled Liz.

Holly, Jeff, and Sean watched helplessly from the ground below.

Suddenly — *"UNNNGGGGH!"* Gorga jerked back, swung around, coughed, clutched his throat, and flailed his spiky tail.

Then right before everyone's eyes, the enormous creature began to shrink!

It was amazing! It was fantastic! It was incredible!

Within minutes, the huge beast shriveled back to its original baby-egg size. It lay quietly in the dust.

The Duffeys came running from the gym.

Liz hopped up from the ground and hugged them. "Mom! Dad! Your recipe worked!"

Mike ran over next to her. "Is that like a speciality of yours, Mrs. D?"

Mrs. Duffey laughed. "My secret diet recipe. Lose weight in seconds!"

Kramer Duffey picked up the tiny lizard-sized dino and stroked its back. "Goo-goo, Gorga. We're going to take you back home."

Then, in one quick move, the world-famous paleontologist leaped over to his dump truck, climbed onto the hood, and shouted, "To the boneyard, dear!"

Mrs. Duffey jumped into the driver's seat, waved to Liz, and roared away into the desert.

"Amazing, isn't it?" said Liz. "This could only happen in Grover's Mill."

Mike turned around and looked up Main Street. "Yeah, Grover's Mill. What's left of it."

Oh, My Town!

Liz turned to look. Grover's Mill was a mess. Nearly every building on Main Street had been stomped flat. Nothing was left standing. It would take years and years to rebuild.

A crowd gathered in front of the school. Holly, Jeff, and Sean joined Liz and Mike.

"Wow," said Mike. "Only one word describes this — smoldering ruin!"

But Liz didn't bother to correct Mike. In that moment, she realized her life had changed forever. "It's like the end of the world!"

A lump started to form in her throat. She felt as if she was going to cry.

Mr. Sweeney, the janitor, came stumbling from the school. "Oh, my town! My town! I loved it so!"

"So did I!" Liz cried out.

Everyone gasped when they heard her.

Liz stepped back. She saw the looks on the faces of her friends. "What? No! I mean . . . Wait, you thought I meant Grover's Mill? Oh, ha-ha, that's so funny. No, I was talking about some other town. Far away from here. Really!"

Errrch!

A long black limousine pulled up. The door swung open and out stepped a man in a tuxedo.

"Principal Bell!" Liz blurted out.

It *was* Mr. Bell, and with him was Miss Lieberman in a long gown. They turned back to the car, and the principal leaned in. "Yes. Yes. Mmm, yes. Of course! Thank you!"

An instant later, the limo was gone.

Liz stepped over to Mr. Bell. "Was that — ?"

"Yes, the President came to inspect the terrible damage. I'm pleased to say that Grover's Mill has been declared a disaster area!"

"Finally," Liz muttered, making sure everyone heard.

Mr. Bell went on. "And the President is so grateful that we stopped the monster here, she's promised that Grover's Mill will be rebuilt as soon as possible!"

"Great!" said Liz. She dug into her backpack. "Let's start by making some changes! I just happen to have a long list of things that — "

But it was already too late.

Before Liz could find her list, a convoy of army trucks roared into town, and — *Bam!-ZZZ!-Clunk!-Whirr!*

Grover's Mill was back.

Down to the last weird detail.

Double Dunk Donut Den.

Usher's House of Pancakes.

W. Reid Elementary School.

And not a single thing was different!

"Now hurry home, children!" boomed Principal Bell with a big smile.

Mrs. Carbonese shuffled over. "And you'll have just enough time to finish your writing contest entries before bedtime! Remember, they're due tomorrow!"

Liz looked at her friends. She sighed a deep sigh. "Come on, guys. There's nothing more to do here. Let's go."

Mike, Holly, Jeff, and Sean walked along with her. No one said anything for a while.

"What was that writing contest again?" asked Mike.

"After a day like today, who remembers?" said Liz.

As they all watched the trucks roar away into the sunset, Liz felt something rumble beneath her feet. She stopped and looked down.

Two tiny red dots winked up at her from a crack in the sidewalk. A second later, they were gone. Liz nodded to herself. Yes, everything was the same:

"I just remembered that contest," said

Mike. "We have to write a paragraph that describes our town."

"That won't be hard," said Liz. "My paragraph would only be three words: The Weird Zone. Period."

"That's four words," said Mike.

Bong! chimed the brand-new donut.

Sssss! sizzled the brand-new pancake pan.